With Deadly Purpose

With Deadly Purpose

John W. Wood

DEDICATION

To all of the men and women who answered the call to arms by their nation and know that war is never over.

VA HOSPITAL

Lieutenant Kramer, nurse, United States Navy, was tired, very tired. She was irritated when she heard hard heels in the darkened hallway. 'Now who can that be,' she wondered, 'no one is supposed to be here this time of night.'

Kramer peered over the counter in front of her desk. A Marine in summer dress uniform with staff sergeant stripes stepped out of the dark. 'My god, the man is huge,' thought Kramer. The Marine stepped up to the counter, "Good evening Lieutenant; I would like to see Sergeant Early."

"How did you get in here? Visiting hours were over hours ago."

He doesn't answer her question. "Ma'am, I'm shipping out in two days. I just found out that Sergeant Early is here. He's my brother-in-law, and I won't be back for some time."

Lieutenant Kramer's eyes were drawn to the Staff Sergeant's display of ribbons and devices. Four stood out, the BUDS (Basic Underwater Demolition/Seal), Parachute (jump qualified), the Silver Star with combat V, and the Purple Heart with a star (two). She had seen them before and knew what they were, but never had she seen them all on the same Marine. "What's your name sergeant?"

"It's Behr, Ma'am; Staff Sergeant Behr."

"Are you a Recon Marine like Sergeant Early?"

"Yes, Ma'am."

"Well, Sergeant Early is sedated and restrained; he won't even know you're here."

"Yes, Lieutenant; but I'll know."

Kramer studied Behr's face, 'Marines…he'll just find a way if I don't let him see him.' "Against my better judgment, you can see him for a few minutes. Don't be shocked when you see him."

Behr's face broke into a smile any Hollywood actor would want to have, "Yes, Ma'am! Thank you."

Kramer picked up her keys and with the touch of a smile said, "It's a Marine thing I suppose, Staff Sergeant Behr?"

"Yes, it's a Marine thing, Lieutenant."

Behr and Lieutenant Kramer began walking; Behr fell-in to the left and a step behind her. He skipped, getting in step with the Navy nurse. Nurse Kramer stood a little straighter while she and the respectful Marine moved along the darkened passage, wondering a little about both these men.

Kramer stopped at a door with a small window. After looking through the window, she fingered through her ring of keys, found one and unlocked the door.

Behr stepped into a stark room containing only a white metal chair, a white nightstand, and a hospital bed. There were no windows. In the bed was Sergeant Early, United States Marine Corps. Behr had a surge of sadness, nearly bringing tears to his eyes. Early wore restraints on his ankles and wrists. Early's pajama top was open exposing bandages, and drainage tubes that led from his body down to covered containers under the bed. Behr's brother-in-law mumbled with his eyes closed.

"He's heavily sedated. His wounds are amazing; he's been shot multiple times, but not one bullet struck a vital organ. He has three broken ribs, and his left leg was fractured, but the doctor was able to save it, and it appears to be healing well."

Nurse Kramer moved to the bed bumped the chair causing the metal chair to screech across the floor. Early, his arms restrained, tried to sit up and when he couldn't he began violently thrashing about. Startled, Kramer backed away, as Behr moved closer. In a commanding voice, Behr said, "Sergeant Early, at ease Marine, that's an order!"

Kramer watched in disbelief as Early stopped thrashing around, his eyes never opening, but his head turning as if he were observing something. Behr moved closer, "It's all right Marine we'll take it from here, you rest."

Slowly Early relaxed and lay back down, his facial features softening, and the mumbling stopped.

Kramer moved in close to Early and checked his tubes and bandages. Satisfied all was well she signaled to Behr that they should leave.

After locking the door to Early's room, she turned to Behr. "Thank you, he could have seriously hurt himself. I'm so sorry that I bumped that chair."

"Things happen; will you tell him I was here when you can? I'm headed out, and I don't expect to be back for some time."

"I'll let him know and thank you."

As Behr walked away down the dark hallway, Lieutenant Kramer called out, "Stay safe."

Behr turned and gave her his Hollywood smile. "Not part of the job description ma'am, but thanks." Behr turned and disappeared down the dark hallway.

BATTLE CREEK MICHIGAN, VA HOSPITAL

On the second floor of the hospital, in an office painted pale green sits Commander Gerald Smith, USN. For over twenty-three years as a Dr. of psychiatry MD, Ph.D., LCSW, MFT, he has worked with servicemen and women with Post Traumatic Stress Disorder. Smith, wearing black horn-rimmed glasses, is surrounded by stacks of files on his desk. He has one open, but he's not really reading. After years of war and wounded minds, Smith is daydreaming about retirement. A knock on the door snaps him back to reality, "Come!"

Dr. Philip Donnelly, also a psychiatrist, enters. He's a short nervous man, in the late stages of balding, a civilian who has become disillusioned with his success in treating PTSD. "Good morning Phil, what brings you around this early in the morning?"

"I understand you are releasing Early, this morning."

"Yes, he's made good progress in his recovery, I think he's ready."

"I hope you're right."

"He's responded well to treatment and hasn't had a flashback in months. He's shown no abnormal flashes of anger or aggression. Yes, I think he's ready." Smith closes the thick file; stenciled across the cover, Early, J.K. USMC.

Phil, with his hands clasped behind him, begins pacing. Smith takes his glasses off and chews on the end of one of the bows. "Early is smart Phil, if he has a problem we're right here."

Phil stops and looks a Smith, "We train these guys to kill, send them to some... some God-forsaken place, and switch em on. Damn it, its hell trying to switch em off!" Phil starts to pace again.

"Phil, I wouldn't discharge him if I thought for a moment he was a danger to himself or the public."

A knock at the door draws their attention, the door opens, and Smith's secretary sticks her head in. "Sergeant Early is here for his appointment."

Smith slips his glasses back on, "Send him in please."

The secretary opens the door wider and says, "You can go in now."

John Early is dressed in civilian clothing; jeans, a blue button-down collared shirt and black spit-shined cowboy boots with riding heels. Early, with the cowboy boots, looks like a six-foot-four Opie Taylor with a scar over his right eye.

Smith smiles as he thinks, 'Who else but a Marine would starch his jeans and have a crease in them sharp enough you could save with them.'

Phil steps over to Early, looks up and extends his hand. "I understand you're getting released today. I wish you well in whatever you decide to do."

Early shakes the doctor's hand, "Thank you, sir."

"And, Early?"

"Yes, sir?"

"Thank you for your service."

"Yes, sir, thank you sir; and thank you for all you have done for me."

As Phil starts out the door, he says to Smith, "I'll talk to you later, Gerry."

"Right; come on in Sergeant Early and have a seat,"

Smith sees that Early looks healthy, happy and relaxed, "You've been with us a year, you've made great progress."

Early replies, "Thank you, sir."

"I understand your wife has moved here?"

"Yes sir, she has. We've found a house out by the lake."

Smith looks down at Early's thick file on his desk then back at Early. "It's important that you take your medication. You need to stay away from situations that could stress you, setting you up for flashbacks." "Yes sir, I'll remember."

Smith stands, extends his hand to Early who also stands and takes Smith's hand and shakes it. "Stop at the secretary's desk, she has your checkout papers. There's also a list of support groups in the area; I hope you'll give at least one of them a try."

"Yes sir, I'll do that."

Early, automatically does an about-face and leaves the room.

Smith picks up the phone. "You can send in the next patient."

* * *

An hour later, Early walks out the front door of the hospital and looks around and then walks across the lot towards a black SUV. The driver's door opens and a slender, long-legged red-haired girl, with a smile that makes her plain face pretty, gets out. "John, over here!" Kay races to John who sweeps her up and off her feet and swings her around. "Hello, Sweetheart," John nearly chokes up as he says, "God, I love you."

Kay nuzzles his neck, laughing at him, causing chills and goosebumps in her Marine. Her hot breath caresses his ear, "Hey Marine, want to have a good time?"

John grins, twists around and holds her tight against him, "Just what did you have in mind?"

Kay kisses him in a deep, passionate way, her body moving slowly against his. John begins to respond back, but Kay pulls away. Coyly, she takes him by the hand and leads him to the SUV. Early is grinning like an idiot as he opens the passenger door for her. Kay gets in; he closes the door and goes to the driver's side. Still grinning, he tosses the keys in the air, catches them, and then enters the SUV. Behind the wheel, John starts the engine, turns to Kay, "I never thought this day would come, let's go home."

MOTEL ROOM - ONE YEAR LATER

Early, is sitting in a chair cleaning a .45 caliber, Para Ordnance P14 pistol. On the table next to his chair are a lamp and a pistol cleaning kit. Sitting on one of the beds is Behr, who is cleaning an identical pistol. On the bed next to Bear are a cleaning kit and a police scanner. They listen to intermittent police radio chatter on the scanner. An open pizza box is on the night table with a half-eaten pizza. Bear stops working on his pistol and looks over at John.

"How's the chest?"

John pressing his hand lightly to his chest replies, "I'm sore as hell. I'll be black and blue for weeks."

Bear goes back to cleaning his pistol, speaking as he works, "We'll have to get you a new vest."

Early begins to reassemble his pistol, he changes the subject, "I'm surprised we haven't heard anything on the scanner."

Behr, holding his pistol in one hand, stretches across the bed and retrieves the scanner. He fiddles with a knob. "I'll turn it up just in case there's some action we should know about."

As Early watches, Behr picks up the scanner Behr turns the knob. This simple movement sends Early into a flash of memory. In Early's mind, a Marine radioman is calling for fire support as red and green tracers flash around him. The radioman's head explodes from a rifle bullet.

Early snaps back to reality; shaken, he turns in the chair, so Behr can't see his shaking hands. Gaining control John asks, "How long do you want to stay here?"

Behr lays his pistol down on the bed and then takes a piece of pizza from the box on the nightstand. He takes a bite, chewing, he thinks, swallows and says, "Tomorrow; tomorrow we'll go over to Kalamazoo and get the supplies."

"We'd better stash some of the cash. We get within a mile of a drug dog, it'll tag us."

Behr stands, finishes off the piece of pizza, "why don't you take a shower first. I'll get the duffel and bring it in. When you're done with the shower, we'll put some ice on that bruise."

Early gets out of the chair and stands. He winces as he pulls his shirt over his head. On his chest is a large, ugly bruise. Scars from his old wounds and surgeries show as white blotches or lines. "Okay, I'll take my shower." Early walks over to the bathroom and the shower, as he enters he says, "Be sure to look around before you get that shit out of the car."

Behr pulls the covers of the bed over the gun, cleaning kit and the scanner and then goes out the door. Parked in front of their room is the black SUV. Behr opens the hatchback; on the floor is a black duffel bag. On top of the bag is a ballistic vest with a bullet hole. Behr sticks his finger in the hole in the vest and thinks about how John was shot.

FOUR HOURS EARLIER

Older neighborhoods in the city of Battle Creek are made up of large, two-story Victorian houses left over from the boom cereal days. An autumn wind is blowing, and it's raining. On a darkened porch of one of the houses two men wear hoodies, their shoulders hunched against the weather. Across the street and down two houses, is a house with the doors and windows boarded up with sheets of plywood. A dirt drive runs alongside the house with a large tree next to the drive. Under the tree is a beat-up panel truck with a black vent protruding from the roof; written on the side in the fading paint is 'GILBERT'S UPHOLSTERY.'

Inside the van, it is illuminated by a red night-light. There is a desk-counter, and the bottom of a periscope can be seen. Two men, with holstered pistols and police badges hooked to their belts, are seated inside. Wind and rain rattle on the van's metal roof.

One of the two cops, wearing a baseball cap turned backward on his head, is looking through the periscope. The other man is taking notes. Periscope man says, "Two more just went in. What the ... can you believe it? The damned wind knocked a tree limb on top of the scope. Ya better go out there and get it off; we need the pictures for the report."

The note taker, grumbling to himself, pulls on a jacket, turns his hat around, turns off the interior light of the van and opens the door. He steps out into the blustery night and closes the van door.

'Well, at least the rain has stopped, but this wind sucks.' The note taker looks up at the vent and sees a tree limb lying on top of the vent. Stepping up onto the bumper, he stretches trying to reach the limb.

Out of the night, two black-clad figures wearing ski masks and gloves move in behind the cop. One points his pistol to the side of the cop's head. Notetaker slowly turns his head; the gunman puts a finger to his lips signaling silence. He then motions to the cop to open the van door.

As Note Taker opens the van door, the gunman pulls him back by the collar as the second man, pistol at the ready, steps into the opening of the van.

Periscope man looks up as the black-clad man comes into the van. The gunman motions for the cop to lie on the van floor. Notetaker reluctantly complies and lies face down on the floor of the van. The gunman removes the cop's pistol, ejects the magazine, and ejects a round from the chamber. He places the pistol and magazine on the desk, takes the handcuffs from the cuff holster on the cop's belt and cuffs the cop's hands behind his back. He removes a roll of duct tape from the cargo pocket of his trousers and rips a piece off and tapes the mouth of the cop and backs out of the van. Notetaker has duct tape on his mouth, and his hands are cuffed behind him. The gunman silently motions to the cop to get into the van and to lie down. He places the cop's empty pistol and magazine on the desk next to the other pistol. He once again signals silence with a finger to his lips, as he and the other man close the van doors they wave goodbye.

The two gunmen move rapidly up the street across from where the two men are standing on the porch. In the shadow of a large tree, Behr pulls up his ski mask. Early pulls his up, pulls back his coat sleeve and looks at his watch. Across the street at the house two people come out, get into an old Buick and drive away. Early pulls his sleeve down and says, "That leaves about six to eight people inside; what do you think?"

Behr pulls his mask down, "Piece of cake."

"Roger that, lets mess em up."

Using the shadow cast by a telephone pole that stretches across the street, to conceal their movements, they run silently towards the house across the street.

On the porch, the two men wearing hoodies face away from the weather; they are both listening to loud rap from their iPods.

John and Behr rapidly move up the porch steps taking the guards completely by surprise. Behr, using an elbow, slams it to the side of the head of one of the men, knocking him unconscious.

Early strikes the second guard in the throat. As the man grabs his throat, Early strikes him under the chin with a vicious uppercut with the heel of his hand. The guard collapses to the floor next to the other man.

Behr moves up to the door, looks back as Early who nods his head.

Behr kicks in the front door, and then with their pistols at the ready, they both quickly enter the house splitting left and right.

* * *

Inside the crack house, two young black men are sitting behind a long folding table. There is a pistol on the table in front of each man. A teenage boy and girl are just turning away from the table when the door crashes open. Two black-clad men, guns in hand, enter breaking left and right. "Everybody, on the floor; get on the floor or you die, on the floor!"

The boy and girl throw themselves to the floor, in terror, the girl begins to weep.

The two black men stand, knocking over their chairs as they pick up their pistols. One of the black men yells, "Not today son-of-a-bitch!"

He shoots John, the bullet strikes John's ballistic vest in the chest area; John staggers but quickly recovers. He fires a triple tap, two to the chest, and one to the head of the shooter.

Behr is distracted by the terrified girl as she tries to stand and run. The boy grabs her and pulls her back to the floor.

One of the dealers points his pistol at Behr. John responds, swings his pistol around and triple taps the second shooter before he can fire.

11

Early and Behr sweep the room with their eyes and guns looking for additional targets.

The girl on the floor is crying uncontrollably. The boy tries to comfort her and to keep her quiet.

Behr motions to the boy and the girl to stay where they are. The Bear stands guard as John moves to the table. Silence falls and is broken only by the sobs of the young girl.

MOTEL - SHOWER

Behr moves the vest to the side and then removes a black duffel bag from the SUV. He closes the hatch. He re-enters the motel room, goes to the bed and dumps the contents of the duffel, which is full of money, onto the bed. Behr sits on the bed and begins sorting and straightening the bills.

In the shower, John stands with his head down, the water beating down on his neck. John's hands tremble. For no evident reason John slaps his hands several times on the wall of the shower. 'What has happened to us,' he cries out in his mind, 'why did you have to die?'

ONE WEEK EARLIER

Small neighborhood bar, the clock over the bar says it ten o'clock. The bartender is a stocky, gray-haired man. He's standing behind the bar washing a glass. John is seated at the end of the bar; slowly turning his beer glass making wet circles on the bar.

The door to the bar opens; Behr, wearing jeans, a muscle-shirt, and sunglasses, stops as the door closes behind him. Removing his sunglasses, Behr sees John at the bar.

Behr reaches into his pants-pocket as he heads towards John and then stands behind him. From his pocket, Behr removes a large bronze coin and tosses it on the bar. The coin wobbles around finally landing face up. The coin has the Marine Corps globe and anchor on the face; written around the edge, Semper Fidelis, USMC. Behr barks out loudly, "Challenge!"

John stares at the coin a moment then swings around on the barstool. His face lights up into a smile "Bear!"

Bear, sounding like a Marine drill instructor says, "Have you've got your coin, Marine?"

John with a smirk stands and reaches into his pocket. He pulls out an identical coin and slaps it on the bar. "Guess you buy, Jarhead."

The bartender, who had been watching, approaches John and Bear. Bear says, "Give me a draft and whatever knucklehead is drinking.

The bartender points at the coins, "May I?" Bear pushes his coin towards the bartender.

"Sure, go ahead," said Bear.

Picking up the coin the bartender looks at both sides. On the opposite side of the coin, in large letters is, 'Death before dishonor.' "Afghanistan," Asks the bartender.

Bear straighten slightly, "Yeah, both of us."

Nodding, the bartender places the coin back on the bar. He holds out his arm turning it so that the underside of his forearm is showing. On his forearm is a faded, tattoo of a Marine globe and anchor. "Vietnam, 1972, Tet Offensive, I'll buy.

"Ooh-Rah," Bear and John say loudly.

The bartender smiles, "Semper Fi," and turns to get the drinks.

Bear pulls out a barstool and sits down. "When did you get into town," asks John. "I thought you were in Columbia."

"Bogota, I was training police officers when I got your message about Kay."

The mention of Kay's name produces a look of despair that distorts John's face.

Bear reached out placing his hand on John's shoulder, "I'm sorry man, I got here quick as I could."

John turns away with his head down hiding his grief.

Bear reaches into his pocket and pulls out a wad of bills. He tosses a ten on the bar and waves off the bartender. "Come on John, let's go home."

The disappointed bartender is left holding two beers as he watches Bear and John leave.

EARLY'S CONDO

Early's condo is well furnished but messy. Newspapers are scattered on the floor, a picture frame on an end table by the couch is face down, a rumpled blanket left bunched up on the couch.

From where he is standing, Bear can see the kitchen through a doorway. Dirty dishes fill the sink, and empty beer bottles clutter the counter. A full medicine container lies on its side.

"You wanna a beer?"

"Yeah, I'll take one."

Early goes into the kitchen, he gets two beers from the fridge. He places one on the counter and opens the other. He sees the medicine container, in his mind he can hear Kay, *"Are you taking your meds? I know you think they're a crutch, but honey; for us Sweetheart, the baby and me."*

Early picks up the container and tosses it into a wastebasket. He opens the second beer and returns to the living room. He finds Bear standing in the middle of the living room, his fists on his hips like a D.I. holding inspection.

"Looks like some kinda animal lives here."

John hands a beer to Bear, "I haven't been able to get it together. I've been sleeping on the couch, can't bring myself to sleep in our bed."

Bear pushes newspapers and the blanket aside and sits on the couch. He looks up at John, "Tell me what happened."

John looks out the sliding glass door; he takes a drink of his beer. "Kay was shopping; she had a month to go before the baby was due."

John moves closer to the sliding glass doors, staring out at the lake. "She'd finished shopping and was going to the car when two guys started shooting it out. They missed each other; But Kay was hit, killed her and the baby."

"They know who did it?"

John turns from the sliding doors, "Cops think it was a drug deal gone bad; they arrested a suspect but couldn't hold him."

Bear takes a drink of his beer. He notices the picture face down on the end table and picks it up.

The picture is of a radiant Kay in a white wedding dress and John in Marine dress blues. Bear carefully stands the picture up on the table. "What are your plans?"

"I've been working undercover for a security company; drugs in the workplace and internal theft cases mostly."

Bear studies John's face. "Would you want to go back with me to Bogota? I can get you a job teaching close quarter combat to the police."

Early's demeanor changes. "No, I've decided to do something else." Early reaches over the back of the couch, and sorts through some discarded newspapers, he finds the page he wants. "Matter of fact, I've already started." John hands the newspaper to Bear.

Bear silently reads the article, '*The unidentified body of a man, who had been shot execution style, was found today on Dickman Road near the airport. Police say they have no suspects, and that the investigation is ongoing.*'

Bear looks up questioningly, "So what's this?"

"That was me; the dead guy? He's the one the police let go."

Bear cannot believe what he's just heard, "You murdered this guy?"

John, his face is now full of rage, "I took his drug money too; figure it'll help finance my mission."

Confused and angry, Bear shouts, "Mission, what mission?"

John grabs a chair and pulls it up to Bear and sits down. He leans forward; he is animated as he speaks. I'm going to find the other man, the other shooter; the one responsible for Kay's death."

Bear just stares at Early, and then with the newspaper clutched in his fist he angrily shakes it at him. "Vigilantes went out with the cowboys and Indians you stupid shit! You'll go to jail forever if they catch you."

John responds in a soft, plaintive voice, "Kay was my wife, your sister. When I got out of the hospital, she was the glue that held me together, she and the baby. They gave me purpose. Now they're gone." Early's face again shows his anguish, his eyes begin to tear, he absently wipes his face with the back of his hand. His hands tremble, and he stands and turns his back to Bear hiding his shaking hands under his arms. "I just couldn't let it go. The police had one of the shooters, but no witness, no evidence, and they had to release him. I miss her so much." But John's demeanor suddenly hardens again, his anger and aggressiveness returning. He faces Bear, his hands have stopped shaking.

In a low menacing voice, he tells Bear, "I'm gonna use all of my training to find that second man; the man who killed Kay and our baby." John returns to the sliding glass doors and stares out at the lake. Outside, he absently watches a lone goose, calling, circling the lake.

Lost in thought, Bear takes a sip of his beer. He again picks up the wedding picture of Kay and John. Bear holds the picture up, and in his mind, he can hear Kay laughing, dancing with John at their wedding.

Bear sets the picture down on the table and looks over at John, staring out the window. Bear's memory goes back six years to a battle scene, its night and Bear has been shot and is trying to crawl to cover. Out of the darkness and under heavy fire, John Early, firing his rifle, and yelling like a madman, zigs, and zags to Bear. Grabbing Bear by his load harness, John pulls Bear to safety. Bear, knowing nothing of John's flashbacks, takes a deep breath and asks, "What are you doing with the dope?"

John, with a questioning look, turns back to Bear. "I leave it for the cops, along with any guns. The money I keep to finance the mission."

Bear stands and joins his brother-law. Together, they look out at the lake. For a moment, Bear watches the lone, calling goose, and then he turns to John and says, "No Killing."

"Only in self-defense," replies John.

"Okay, ... you can count me in on one condition. After we find Kay's killer, we head for Columbia."

John, too emotional to speak, nods yes and then turns and faces the glass door. Side by side, he and Bear, look out over the lake as the sun drops behind the horizon.

MOTEL - SHOWER

Early takes his hands from the wall of the shower and looks at them. They've stopped shaking. He turns off the water and reaches for a towel.

THE CRACK HOUSE

The rain was that autumn kinda rain that Michigan gets. It doesn't look like much, but it will soak you through and through and chill you to the bone. Outside the Crack House, now outlined with yellow crime-scene tape, uniformed police officers stand in the rain holding spectators and news people back. A patrol unit pulls up to the curb with its light bar lit up. The door opens, and Lieutenant Galloway, looking like life has beaten the crap out of him, gets out of the vehicle. A cigarette dangles from his mouth and is immediately soaked by the rain. Galloway throws the soggy smoke to the ground. As he grinds the soggy butt with the toe of his shoe, a voice says cheerfully, "Divine intervention L. T., you're being told to quit."

Galloway turns to the source of the voice, Sergeant Billings who is a black man with sad eyes, and a wry smile. At forty, Billings is buff and wears his police uniform well. He has a flashlight in his left hand. "Screw you Billings, what've we got?"

Billings begins the litany of his report. At approximately 0135, a shots-fired call came for the 200 block of Ash. Everyone else was tied up, so I took the call. I arrived at approximately 0140 hours. At first, I didn't hear or see anything. Then I observed the van parked across the street. Billings points across the street with his flashlight, illuminating the van parked under the tree. Using his hand to demonstrate, Billings continues, "I observed the van rocking back and forth. As I approached the van, I heard a call for help."

Galloway's head comes up, "A call for help?

"Yeah,"Get us the hell out-a-here," is actually what I heard. Inside the van, I found detectives, White and Osborn handcuffed on the floor of the van."

"You've got to be shitting me!"

Billings shakes his head no. "They'd been gagged with duct tape, but Osborn worked his gag off.

"Where are they now?"

"They weren't injured, so one of the patrol units took them to the station."

Galloway walks over to the van, Billings follows. "Osborn said he went out to remove a fallen limb from the periscope when he was jumped." Billings points to the ground with the beam of his flashlight. "You can see where the Perps were waiting."

Galloway sees what is left of the fading footprints in the wet mud.

Billings then shines his flashlight into the limbs of the tree illuminating a limb with a fresh break on one end. "Perps put the branch over the periscope to get the Narcs to open the door." Billings moves the beam of his light to the top of the van and the periscope. A broken tree limb lies on top of the periscope. "The Perps were masked and dressed like SWAT; both carried what looked like forty-five autos."

Galloway opens the back of the van, looks inside and then closes the door.

"What happened next?"

"Both White and Osborn say they heard shots a couple minutes later then nothing until I showed up."

Galloway nods his head at the house. "What about the house?"

"Let's go over, I think Forensics has finished, and the Coroner is on his way." Galloway and Billings cross the street; officers greet them as they pass. News people shout out questions at Galloway who ignores them. The two officers climb the steps to the front door which is guarded by a huge, uniformed police officer. The officer hands Galloway, a clipboard. Galloway takes the board, signs it and writes the time and then hands it to Billings. Billings signs it and hands it back to the officer. The door opens, and the Crime Scene Investigator steps out. The CSI is a short, bird-like young man with glasses who is irritatingly exuberant. "Hey L. T., you want me to take you through it?"

Galloway looks trapped but says, "Yeah, show me what you've got."

Billings smiles at Galloway's reaction to the CSI, who is oblivious to the Lieutenant's unease. Galloway and Billings follow the CSI into the house. Lying on the floor, behind a table are the bodies of two black men. Both have bullet wounds to the head and chest. The CSI stops next to the bodies. "The two Vics have ID from Detroit." The CSI squats next to the bodies. With his pen, he points out their bullet wounds. "Each man received a triple tap, two to the chest, and one to the head. The CSI looks up at Galloway, "Very professional. The only brass I found was a nine mill." The CSI holds up an evidence bag with a shell casing in it. "But from the damage done to our Vics, I'd say the shooters used forty or forty-fives. We'll know more after the autopsy. The Vics are the only people we found in the building. White and Osborn said the place had light but steady traffic when this went down."

Galloway looks around the room, steps around the bodies and inspects the table.

On the table are two pistols and a sawed-off shotgun, each neatly positioned behind the boxes. Pasted on the table is a yellow circle with a SMILEY FACE. Galloway turns to the CSI. "You do this; lay it out all nice and neat?"

"Nope found it that way."

The CSI enthusiastically asks, "See the smiley face on the table?"

Galloway frowning ignores the question. Instead, he reaches into his shirt pocket and pulls out his smokes. He shakes one out, and places it unlit, between his lips. He absently pats his pockets as he continues to examine the table. "Find any money?"

"Not a penny. Did find dope, it's in the boxes."

Galloway glances into a box, and then turns to Billings, "I want every crackhead you can find talked to; someone saw what happened here."

"I'm already on it L.T."

Galloway speaks in a commanding voice to the energetic CSI. "I don't want any talk about vigilantes."

The CSI who seems oblivious to the order replies, "But there's the smiley sticker and the dope."

Galloway is visibly irritated by the CSI's personality and his remarks. But a call comes across his portable radio, just as he's going to speak. "L.T., the Chief wants you to 1019 the station."

"10-4 dispatch, E.T.A. about ten." Galloway faces Billings and the CSI. His face has a no-nonsense look, "I'm headed back to the station, remember, I want no talk of vigilantes. I don't want the press turning this into a circus."

Billings and the CSI nod their heads and then watch as Galloway heads out the door.

Outside, Galloway stops outside of the door, finds his lighter and lights his cigarette; blowing a cloud of smoke into the wet air. The huge officer at the door grimaces as he fans the air with his hand, irritating Galloway. Galloway pockets his lighter as he stomps down the steps and off the porch.

Inside the house, the CSI turns to Billings. Excitedly he says to Billings, "It's them, isn't it?"

Now Billings is irritated by the zealous CSI, "You heard the L.T., knock it off!"

The CSI looks like a scolded puppy. Billings leaves the house and stands on the front porch. He watches, as Galloway's patrol car pulls away. His attention is grabbed by the huge cop at the door who is still fanning the smoky air with his hand. Shaking his head, Billings quickly moves down the steps and out to his patrol car.

SMOKE'S HOUSE

Smoke, a well-muscled, handsome black man is in his twenties. Stripped to the waist, he is working out on an exercise machine; his ripped muscles bulge with the effort.

Standing in nervous silence is The Bean, a painfully thin, unattractive black man, in his late twenties. He is obviously in awe of Smoke.

Smoke, finishing his reps on the machine, sits up and pulls a towel from the back of the machine. Wiping the sweat from his face and chest, he watches Bean from the corner of his eye. Smoke enjoys intimidating Bean. "How come you ain't out doing collections," demands Smoke.

The Bean spits out his words, "It's them, vigilantes, again! They killed the two guys from Detroit, took all the money. The cops got the dope, Smoke, they got all of it."

Smoke glares at Bean. Bean fidgets nervously under Smoke's gaze. "You sure it was them," asks Smoke.

"A crack-head said it was two guys dressed like SWAT. He said they just shot them boys dead quick as you please."

Smoke absently wipes at his face and chest with the towel, "They black or white?"

"Not sure, they were dressed in black with black ski masks and gloves. But the crack-head thought maybe they were white."

Smoke stands, drapes the towel around his neck, hanging onto the ends as he thinks. "I want more soldiers at the houses. You start making pickups more often." Smoke pulls a cell phone from his pocket, stops and says to Bean. "Detroit has some people used to be in the Army Special Forces. I think if these vigilantes want war; I'll give em a war."

Hesitantly Bean asks, "Smoke, do you think this could have anything to do with the guy that shot at you? I mean, shit man, everything's been screwed since then."

Smoke thinks back to that day of the shootout. In a store parking lot, an angry Smoke has discovered a scratch on the door of his BMW.

A shot explodes, and a bullet strikes close to Smoke's head. Smoke ducks and drawing his pistol he begins shooting. In the background, police sirens can be heard. Smoke quickly enters his car and then speeds away. To Bean Smoke says, "Two things I know. I don't know the guy that shot at me, but I'll wax his ass, I ever see him again."

Smoke then dismisses Bean, with a wave of his hand. Bean leaves, as Smoke connects on his cell. "This is Smoke, it happened again. I need them two army dudes you told me bout."

EARLY'S HOUSE

John's kitchen has been cleaned up, the dishes put away, no newspapers litter the floor, the blanket is still on the couch but is folded. On the kitchen table are several 5"X 2" X 4" wooden blocks. Also on the table, a pile of plastic bags full of electronics and nine-volt batteries. There is a screwdriver, a small drill and a sack of small wood screws.

Clamped to the end of the table is a small vice, with a block of wood in it. John has just finished cutting the block in half edgeways, with a saw. Removing the two pieces, John hands them to Bear.

Bear has a small electric hand tool, and he begins hollowing out the two halves of the block. As Bear finishes one half, he hands it back to John, who drills a small hole in the side. John blows the sawdust out of the hole. Picking up a packet of electronics he carefully places them in the cavity and then connects a 9-volt battery.

Finished grinding out the other half of the block Bear hands it to John. John fits the two sides together, picks up a screwdriver and four screws. He then screws the two sides together.

Bear stands up, dusting off the sawdust. "Let's give em a try."

John picks up the assembled blocks and takes them outside onto the deck. Bear turns on a police scanner. "OK, give me a short count!"

Out on the deck, John picks up a block and speaks into the small hole drilled in the block, "Testing, short count; One, two, three, three, two, one."

Bear holds police scanner that has an earpiece plugged into it and the earpiece in his ear. He can clearly hear John's short count, "Testing, short count; one, two, three, three two, one."

"OK, try the next one."

After checking all the blocks, John rejoins Bear in the kitchen. Bear goes to the refrigerator and retrieves two beers. He opens them and hands one to John.

"Where'd you learn the trick with the blocks?"

"An under-cover I worked with used to be in Special Forces. He showed me. Each block is on a separate, voice-activated frequency. We place these say along a sidewalk. As a talker moves, the scanner picks up the transmission from the next block."

Bear starts stacking the blocks, "I've been thinking, maybe we'd better start doing some counter surveillance. I'm sure the police and maybe even the dealers, will start doing some of their own."

"I know the dealers have some guys like us working for them. I heard the State Narcs talk about em."

"You said your boss is in tight with the PD, how about you pay him a visit; maybe you can get a feel for what's going on."

"Roger that, I'll go in tomorrow. I owe them a visit anyway; I'll go first thing tomorrow."

PAINFUL REMEMBRANCE

The sliding glass door opens, and John steps out onto the deck. Geese are calling, as they circle the lake.

From inside the kitchen, Bear calls out, "You want another beer?"

"Nah, I'm good!"

In the kitchen, Bear drinks his beer as he looks through the window. He watches Early briefly, and then he moves from the kitchen to the living room. On the end table is the wedding picture. Bear salutes the picture with the bottle, "Semper Fi, Kay."

Outside, John is standing, his hands gripping the railing. On the lake, the sun is beginning to set. On the lake, someone starts a boat motor. The deep throaty sound echoes across the lake triggering a flashback. Like a bad dream, John can hear a gas generator noisily running outside a tent next to the entrance of a cave. A Taliban guard, his AK-47 slung over his shoulder, is smoking a cigarette. John attacks the guard from behind, driving his knife into the guard's back. The guard falls to the ground face up. John groans grabbing his head as he fights his loss of the moment.

The sound of the motorboat has frightened the geese, and the flock flies into the air calling to each other. The motor is turned off. The geese are circling, calling, and then glide back onto the lake. John, his hands gripping his head, sits down heavily onto a deck chair. Head-in-hand, he sits in the dark returning to reality.

In the living room, Bear sits on the couch drinking his beer. He feels tired; he pulls a wallet from his hip pocket and opens it. Bear looks at a photograph of himself and a woman, Carlotta. She has long black hair, possesses a mature beauty. She appears to be of Spanish - Indian descent. In the picture, Bear has his arm around her waist. Bear and the woman are smiling. They appear to be happy.

Bear smiles as he remembers; he and Carlotta are in bed. Bear spoons Carlotta, his arms wrapped around her. Bear kisses her on her bare shoulder. Hidden from Bear, Carlotta's face is sad, but she smiles and closes her eyes, as Bear kisses her. Without turning, she asks in Spanish, "When will you leave?"

"I have a flight out day after tomorrow."

"You'll be gone long?"

"No, my sister is buried; there is nothing more I can do now. But John, he's all the family I have left."

"This John, he is a good man?"

"He's the best; we met in the Marines."

Bear lets go of Carlotta as he rolls onto his back. Carlotta turns to him, wraps her arm around him, and places her head on his chest. Absently, Bear massages her back, Carlotta snuggles, luxuriating in the attention.

Bear grins, "John was such an asshole; you know, I had to kick the shit out of him to finally get his attention.

Carlotta raises her head and looks at Bear, "He is your friend, and you beat him up?"

"Ah, it's a Marine thing."

"But he changed, he married your sister."

"Yeah, he changed, John became a damned fine Marine, his men respected him."

"You introduced him to your sister?"

"Oh, hell no; Kay came to visit me on the base one day. I've heard of love at first sight, but that day I saw it happen. John and I were in the Enlisted Men's club when she walked in. John looked up, saw Kate and immediately stood up and pulled out a chair for her. They spent the whole meal talking and looking at each other as if I wasn't even there."

"It sounds so romantic."

"I sure as hell didn't think so at the time, but John treated Kate with respect; you know, like a man does who really loves someone."

Carlotta hugs Bear, her cheek rests on his chest, "You go, you take care of your friend. I'll be here for you." Bear hugs her, kissing her forehead.

On the couch, Bear closes the wallet.

Outside on the deck, the sun casts shadows across the lake. John Early sits at peace for the moment as he watches a lone goose circling the lake, calling.

MURDERER

In an office building in downtown Battle Creek, John skips the elevator and runs up several flights of stairs testing his breath and heart rate. On the fifth-floor landing, he stops, waits for his breath to calm and then opens a door. He steps into a hallway. John places two fingers on the side of his neck as he looks at his watch. John smiles and then continues down the hall. He stops in front of an office door with a frosted glass window. CARLYLE & ASSOCIATES is printed in black letters, on the glass; printed in smaller black lettering below the company name, ENTER. Early opens the door and goes in.

Inside the office area one desk and three chairs, several file cabinets and a small table with a Mr. Coffee and service. Displayed on the wall are a state of Michigan Private Investigator and a Private Security licenses. There are no personal items in the office or on the desk. A closed door to the left of the desk has a sign that reads Private. Behind the desk sits Millie Carlyle, a handsome woman with red hair, who is in her forties. There's a hardness about her that disappears when she sees John enter the office and she smiles.

"Hi Millie, is the boss in?"

Millie is obviously happy to see John, "He's on the phone, should be clear soon. Want a cup of coffee, I just made it."

John goes to the coffee table; picks up a Styrofoam cup and pours a cup of coffee. He takes his coffee to a chair next to Millie's desk and sits down.

Millie has stopped typing and turns her full attention to John.

"Anything going on," asks John.

"Just, same old, same old. We may get another corporate job. They're talking about a couple of undercovers and several cameras."

The door marked private opens and Carlyle comes into the room. Carlyle is in his late forties, average height, his black hair is neatly combed and parted, and he's beginning to thicken around the middle. But he still has a boyish look and a great smile. In his hand, Carlyle has several sheets of paper.

"Hey John, it's good to see you."

"Have you got a few minutes?"

"Sure, go on in my office, I'll be right back." Carlyle turns to Millie and hands her the papers in his hand. "You can get the contract ready. I'm to meet with their personnel guy tomorrow."

John gets up and goes into Carlyle's office. On one wall is a framed Detroit paper page showing Carlyle and Millie, both in Detroit Police uniforms, smiling for the camera. Millie is a sergeant and Carlyle is a Lieutenant. The headline reads, Two of Detroit's finest, wedded.

There are other pictures of Millie and Carlyle, in uniform and civilian clothes. There is a photograph of them on a dock, smiling, fishing rods in hand, and standing next to two large sailfish. Millie's fish is larger than Carlyle's.

Carlyle enters the office and takes a seat behind the desk, "Have a seat John, what's up?"

John takes the chair in front of Carlyle's desk. He takes a sip of his coffee. "I'm going to be out of the loop for a while. The V.A. wants me to go in for counseling."

"John, take as much time as you need."

Bear, Kay's brother, is in town, he's staying with me."

"Bear," asks Carlyle.

Yeah, his name is spelled B-e-h-r. But you know the Corps, wasn't long before he became The Bear."

"You all right financially, anything we can do to help?

"I'm good, I've got my disability and some money put away, but thanks. Hope I haven't put you in a bind."

"Hell don't worry about it. You'll have a job when you're ready to come back."

"Roger that, and thanks," John finishes his coffee, tosses the cup in a wastebasket next to the desk. "Have you heard anything more about the shooting?"

"Only that one of the suspects was shot and killed. The investigator on the case said the dead guy couldn't have done it. His alibi checked out, he was nowhere near the scene."

Shaken by the information John sees in his mind's eye the suspect is on his back, his arms extended in a defensive posture, he's crying. "Man, I didn't do it. I don't even own a gun!"

John's hands begin to tremble; he drops them low, so the desk hides them. He eyes the wastepaper basket, sure he's going to throw up.

Carlyle doesn't seem to notice. "I did hear that the PD has a new suspect, a black guy named Williams; his street-name is Smoke."

John is interested but is still stressed. John stands, and then goes to the window and looks out, his back to Carlyle.

"The detective told me Smoke is also a suspect in two other killings. They can put him in the area the day Kay was shot."

Taking a deep breath, John turns back to face Carlyle. He has changed, the warrior is back.

"This Smoke, is he a local? I've never heard of him."

"I only know what I've heard. He's from Detroit, has a rep as a real bad-ass, tries to keep a low profile. That's about all I know about him."

Anxious to leave, John says, "I appreciate your help; I'll get back to you and let you know how things are going."

Carlyle remains seated as John reaches over the desk and shakes hands with him.

As John leaves Carlyle's office, he stops at Millie's desk. "See you Millie and thanks."

"See you, John, keep in touch." John waves and is out the door. Millie watches him leave then stands and goes into Carlyle's office; she takes the chair in front of the desk. "So?"

"He's going out to the VA for counseling; say's Kay's brother is staying with him."

"He's lost his buddies in that damned war, and now his wife and child; I hope he can keep it together."

"I just hope he doesn't take it into his head to do something about it."

"You said Kay's brother is staying with him?" Carlyle nods his head yes.

"I'm sure he'll watch over him. Keep him from doing something stupid."

SHARE-A-RIDE PARKING LOT

Smoke is in the driver's seat of a new black BMW watching traffic as it splashes by in the rain.

A Black Lexus pulls off the highway and enters the lot and parks next to Smoke. Two men, one an African American, the other Caucasian, exit the passenger side of the Lexus. The two men are big, dressed like models from GQ Magazine. They project confidence that some incorrectly perceive as arrogance. Smoke hits the button that pops the trunk lid of his BMW.

The trunk of the Lexus opens, and the two men remove two black, obviously heavy, duffel bags from the trunk. They walk to the back of Smoke's car, open the BMW trunk wider and place the bags inside. The black man tries to slam the self-closing trunk lid. Realizing his mistake, he allows it to close on its own. The white man says something that makes them both laugh. They open the back door of Smoke's BMW and are still laughing as they take their seats in the back.

Smoke is pissed; he looks back at his passengers in the rearview mirror. "What the hell man, you trying to tear the damned lid off the trunk?"

The laughter stops, the black man's face turns menacing. "Chill, I didn't mean no harm."

Suddenly Smoke feels uneasy as he looks at the two in the rearview mirror. He regains control of his anger. With a wave of his hand, he says, "Forget it, I hate driving in this shit; I get all wound-up. You got all your stuff?"

With a smirk, the white guy says, "Yeah man, we're good to go." He winks at the black guy.

Smoke looks out the passenger window. He watches as the Lexus pulls out and then heads back on to the highway. Smoke then pulls out of the lot to the ramp marked Battle Creek and merges onto the highway. Smoke looks into the rearview mirror and continues the conversation. "So, I hear they call you guys the Dynamic Duo, in Detroit."

The black guy says without humor, "Yeah, you can call us Black-man and Rob-em." Rob-em, chuckles, Black-man doesn't.

"Detroit says you were Special Forces, that right?"

Black-man replies, "Eight years, both of us in A-teams."

"So how do you want to handle this?"

Black-man says, "We'll want to look at each one of your locations. We'll go from there."

"Is there anything else you need?"

"Just a car and a place to stay, for right now," says Black-man.

"Already got you a car and a place," Smoke looks in rearview mirror, "I want these so-called Vigilantes, and I want them big time!"

Rob-em coldly responds, "Don't sweat it man; they're as good as got; it's what we do." Smoke understands he could be the target if things don't go well. Detroit told him 'get this thing done or else.'

BATTLE CREEK POLICE DEPARTMENT - NIGHT

Lieutenant Galloway's office is small, with a gray metal desk, and two chairs. It's only redeeming factor, it has a window that looks out onto a city street. On the walls are several certificates for schools and a college diploma for a Master's in Business Administration. There are stacks of files and loose papers on his desk. On the corner of the desk is a portrait of Galloway, two young men, and an attractive woman. Galloway sits behind the desk in a swivel chair that squeaks and has seen better days. Galloway looks at the picture. Unconsciously he reaches for the ring finger of his left hand as to twist a ring. There is only a white band of flesh where a ring once was.

Galloway opens a desk drawer, takes out a bottle of antacid tablets, shakes several out and pops them into his mouth. He begins chewing as he swivels in his chair looks out the window at the rain. His thoughts are about the woman in the picture on his desk.

The woman is Beatrice, Galloway's wife. Galloway is in his police uniform standing in their bedroom while Beatrice is dressed in a nightgown; Beatrice is angry. "Three in the morning; your day off and you're going back in? Is the damn world going to stop when you die?"

Billings enters Galloway's office; he sees the bottle of antacids on the desk. "Hey L.T. looks like you're enjoying your lunch again."

Galloway turns in his chair to face Billings. He asks, "Shouldn't you be on the road protecting the city?"

37

Billings closes the office door then takes a seat in front of Galloway's desk. "I found someone who saw the crack house shooting go down." Galloway perks up and shows immediate interest.

"He said, one of the dealers got off a shot and hit one of the Perps right in the chest." Billings points to his chest indicating the place on his chest with his finger. "The Perp, he takes out the shooter and, then... He then shoots the second dealer, when the dealer tries to shoot his partner!"

Galloway sits thinking, turns away and looks out the window at the rain and the passing traffic. He turns back to Billings. "You don't suppose we have a couple of bad cops, do you?"

"It's crossed my mind. I mean, how many men could take a hit, and then return accurate fire?"

Galloway looks at his watch. "I've got a staff meeting; let's go over this after the meeting."

"I've got a lead on a second possible witness. I'll check it out; maybe have more for you after your meeting."

"Right, keep safe," Galloways says as Billings starts to leave.

Billings touches the brim of his cap with the forefinger of his right hand in a casual salute and then leaves the office.

Galloway turns back to his window and the rain for a moment, thinking how tame this storm is in comparison to those of the monsoon in Vietnam. Turning in his chair, he stands and leaves his office.

POLICE STATION - CONFERENCE ROOM

Galloway enters the conference room. Chief of police White and two other men, one in uniform, Commander Bender, and one in plain clothes, Detective Lieutenant Barns are already seated. The Chief of Police is a large black man, in his fifties, with a shaved head and a deep bass voice. He looks dapper in his business suit.

The Chief stands leans on the conference table on his closed fists, his bull-like neck extended. The other men know the look. He is not pleased.

"This vigilante thing is out of hand. Hell, we don't even know what these guys look like. Now I've got the news people rooting around." The chief with squinted eyes looks at each of the men at the table. His voice starts out low growing in volume as he speaks. He growls "I don't like news people rooting around, especially when I don't know what the hell's going on!"

Galloway speaks up, "What we do know chief is that these two are probably professionals. By that I mean they're well trained like police, or maybe military."

Chief White straightens up and eyes Galloway, "You're saying we've got a couple of bad cops?"

If they're cops, I don't think they're from here. I just can't imagine anyone from our department who would do this."

The officers around the table nod their heads in agreement. Galloway continues, "We know the Perps are well trained. Hell, one was reportedly shot, and then took out two shooters without blinking an eye."

The detective Lieutenant says with sarcasm, "Stoned, probably didn't feel a thing."

Shaking his head, Galloway responds, "I don't think so. Perp did a triple tap on both shooters. Stoned people don't shoot like that."

Chief White, his frustration growing, says, "I want these guys ASAP. I don't want them in our town. I don't want a drug war in our town." Leaning again on the table, he growls again, "Get em."

EARLY'S CONDO - BEDROOM - MORNING

The door to the bedroom is closed, but light can be seen seeping in under the door. Next to the bed an alarm clock, its irritating alarm jabs at the sleeping Bear. Bear, in shorts and a T-shirt, rolls over and eyes the clock. He turns off the alarm and sits on the edge of the bed. He stands and stretches and opens the door and walks out. The smell of fresh perked coffee wafts through the air. Bear heads for the kitchen.

When Bear walks into the kitchen, John dressed in black sweats, is pouring himself a cup of coffee. He greets Bear with, "You gonna run this morning?"

"Yeah, but first I need coffee."

Walking to the cupboard Bear gets a cup, goes to the pot and pours a cup of coffee.

"I thought we'd go into town and run on the Linear. We can get the lay of the land as we run."

Bear a cup of coffee halfway to his lips asks, "Linear?"

The Linear Park, it's a paved trail that circles the city. We'll park at the junior college and start from there."

Bear takes a drink of coffee; and then he starts walking to the door, "I'll get dressed."

A half-hour later, the two Marines are standing next to the black SUV parked in the driveway. In the drive next door is a green van with the sliding side door open. A young woman is buckling a baby into a car seat in back as two young school-age children sit in the van waiting.

The older children see the two men. They wave and in unison call out, "Hi Mr. Early!"

Early and Bear stop and look back. The mother looks up from the baby, "Good morning John, how are you doing?"

"I'm good, thank you. Say, this is my brother-law. Bear, this is Jean, our neighbor."

Jean looks at the huge man dressed in black sweats, "Bear?"

"Behr ma'am but yes, they call me Bear."

Jean smiles, "Nice to meet you, but I have to run. For some reason, we're running late. You guys have a great day." John stares at the baby in the baby seat. Jean closes the sliding doors remotely; the van door slowly hiding the child from John's sight. As Jean backs past John and Bear, the Children wave at them. John stands silent, watching the van disappear around a corner.

In the SUV, Bear asks, "Is Jean married? I don't remember seeing another car parked at her house."

"Her husband was killed by a drunk driver last year. The drunk was driving a stolen car; he'd just gotten out of prison. There was only the life insurance from her husband. It wasn't much, she been living on a teacher's salary."

"Jesus, you just never know do you, she seems to be really nice."

"Yeah, she and Kate got to be good friends."

LINEAR PARK - JUNIOR COLLEGE PARKING LOT

John pulls into an empty space and parks. The weather is again misting rain. Bear and John, get out of the SUV, and using the side of the vehicle for balance, they stretch their hamstrings. Bear does not appear pleased with the Michigan fall weather. John continues stretching but looks over at Bear and grunts a laugh. "Come on Bear, it's not that bad, you'll get used to it."

Bear, standing on one leg, grabs the ankle of the other and pulls it up, "With all the VA hospitals in the country why did you pick this one?"

"I didn't, Battle Creek VA was the closest hospital for guys with Post Traumatic Stress. After my wounds healed, they sent me here."

Bear stands flat footed and touches his toes. "Kay wrote me once, told me she liked it here, you?

John, his hands behind his head does several twists. "Yeah, it's kinda like Kentucky, lots of rednecks and the hunting's good."

Looking up at the misting sky, and around at his surroundings, Bear shrugs his shoulders, and then tugs his hood forward and over his head. "Where do we go from here?"

John pulls his hood over his head, points with his chin to a path leading down a hill to a paved path. "We'll head that way. There's a loop that will bring us back here, about five miles total."

John and Bear head down the path, moments later, in the distance the path curves; there are bushes that prevent seeing around the curve. From behind the bushes, a girl in a spandex running suit rushes towards them. She is not jogging, she is running, and fear is written all over her face.

Around the curve comes first one man, tall and skinny, he's grinning. In a moment, two more men, not as agile as the first come and it's obvious they are chasing the girl. Looking back over her shoulder, the girl stumbles and falls. The first man runs up on the girl. She begins to kick and scream as the attacker tries to grab her. She is putting up a good fight, but the other two men, now laughing, are running to help their buddy.

The look on John's face turns deadly. Without speaking, using hand signals, he indicates Bear is to take the two. Bear puts on a burst of speed while John attacks the man after the girl. As John approaches, the attacker is on top of the girl. John calls out, "Hey, asshole!"

The attacker looks up, surprised. A running kick to the face from John sends the attacker sprawling, then with blinding speed, John is on him beating him with elbow blows and the heels of his hands. The bloodied attacker groans and then unconscious, he collapses.

Down the path, the two accomplices see Bear rushing towards them. They also see their friend on the ground receiving a stunning beating. They turn to run but too late, Bear is on them.

Bear slams into one knocking him into the other man making them both fall to the ground.

The closest man to Bear immediately tries to stand, but Bear throws a sidekick to his head, blood and teeth fly from the attacker's mouth. He collapses to the ground. The second man also tries to stand, but Bear takes him to the ground by stomping on the back of his knee. Bear rains devastating blows to the head and body knocking him unconscious. Standing, Bear looks for more threats and finding none heads back towards John and the girl.

The first attacker Bear kicked, is now on his hands and knees trying to stand. As Bear passes the man, he throws a sidekick to the head dropping him without missing a step. Bear jogs back to John and the girl.

As Bear arrives, he hears John trying to console the frightened girl. "It's all right, they won't hurt you. You're safe now. Is your car parked in the lot?"

The girl nods yes. "I was so scared, I don't know what would have happened if you hadn't come along. John helps her to her feet. "We'll walk you to your car, but you know you shouldn't run without a partner. It's safer with one." John points to Bear, and says, "See, I run with one."

The wide-eyed girl looks at the grinning Bear, then at the unconscious attackers. She tries to smile.

John and Bear escort the girl to the parking lot and her car. Bear says, "We have our car parked in the other direction. We'd better head back, or we'll be late for work."

The girl gets into her car and locks the doors. She watches as John and Bear disappear down the hill. She hears someone yell, "Ooh-rah!"

Pulling out her cell phone the girl calls 911.

Down on the trail, Bear and John stop at each of the still unconscious attackers. Then they continue jogging, disappearing around the curve in the path as in the distance, the wail of sirens can be heard.

POLICE STATION - EVENING

Billings enters Galloway's office. "We might have a break on the Vigilantes. This morning two men saved a college student from muggers on the Linear Park.

"I heard about it., What's that got to do with the Vigilantes?"

"When the responding officers arrived, the three muggers were still at the scene, unconscious."

Billings takes a seat in front of the desk. "All three looked like they'd been in the same car wreck, and guess what? Each one had a smiley face pasted on his forehead."

Galloway leaned forward in his swivel chair, excitement in his tone as he said, "You have got to be shitting me, a smiley face? Did anyone talk to them?"

The Vic, she said they were tall, white, maybe around mid-thirties." Galloway, his head down, is listening. "Both wore black sweats with hoodies, so she couldn't really see their faces. Oh yeah, they both had southern accents."

There is silence as Galloway lifts his head and looks up at Billings from the corner of his eye. The volume of his voice starts low and then rises as his head comes up. "That's it? White, with southern accents, now that narrows it down! Oh hell yes, and don't forget the smiley faces."

Billings has an "I've got something better to tell," look on his face. "Oh yeah, the Vic also said that she heard one of them yell,"Ooh-rah," as they were leaving."

Galloway who is now facing Billings, as he asks, Marines, you think they're Marines?"

"We know the perps are well trained. Who else but a couple of Marines would have the stones to take on the drug trade alone?" Now Billings is smiling, he's enjoying himself.

"Don't you give me that Marine crap, you guys stick together even if you're outlaws, you're some kinda, some kinda cult!"

Billings feigns a look of hurt feelings as he places his hand to his chest, "Gee L.T., you had your chance to be a Marine, but you chose to be an Army of one." Billings grins.

Galloway slowly shakes his head feigning sadness, "You are a sick man Sergeant Billings. If it weren't for the fact that you owe me ten dollars for golf, I'd put you out of your misery."

"Thanks, L.T.; you've always been good to me. In appreciation, I will go and do an extra good job for you."

"Yeah, well while you're out there, ask around about two redneck Marines that think they're superheroes."

Billings touches the brim of his cap with his forefinger in a casual salute and leaves.

In the police parking lot, patrol cars are parked inside a fenced compound. Billings pulls his keys from his pocket as he approaches his patrol car. Two cars down, the head of a young officer can be seen over the top of a patrol vehicle, "Hey sarge, Semper Fi!"

Billings, his back to the officer turns, smiles and shouts, "Ooh-Rah, stay safe." Billings gets into his vehicle, starts the engine, and then starts to back up. A patrol car's horn sounds and Billings stops and lets it pass by. The passing taillights trigger a memory, 1991 somewhere in Kuwait. Billings is in a Humvee on the passenger side. A fifty-caliber machine gun is mounted on top of the vehicle. It is manned by a second Marine; a third Marine is driving. A second Humvee is ahead of them just passing a parked civilian vehicle. The civilian car's tail lights flash, and the car explodes in a fireball. The blast sends the second Humvee into the air and onto its side. It catches fire. The night is suddenly alive with tracers, as weapons are fired by ambushers from the rooftops. The big fifty, on Billings' vehicle, begins firing. Bricks and bodies begin to fly apart, and off the buildings as the gunner fires the fifty at the ambushers. Billings opens the door of his Humvee, gets out, slams the door shut, and fires his rifle at the rooftops as he runs to the burning Humvee. Bullets strike all around Billings, as he tries to pull the screaming, burning men, out of the vehicle. Another explosion knocks Billings to the ground unconscious.

Billings sits in his stopped patrol vehicle staring straight ahead. A horn toots several times, causing Sergeant Billings to look in his rearview mirror. Behind him is another patrol vehicle, blocked by Billings' patrol car. The driver holds his hands up with a questioning look.

Waving his hand, Billings pulls out onto the street.

THE HOOD - EVENING

Bear and John are dressed in dark clothing with hoodies that hide their faces, walking along a sidewalk. Covertly they drop or toss wooden blocks into bushes and along the edge of the sidewalk in front of a house. Finished, the two return to the SUV. They sit slouched, in their seats watching through mono-lens night vision devices held to their eye. Each man holds a police scanner with an earpiece in his ear listening.

* * *

Billings, on patrol, is driving past a donut shop parking lot. Three cars are parked side by side. One is a black Cadillac. Billings pulls into a parking spot next to the Cadillac. Through the window, he can see Carlyle seated alone in a booth. Billings parks his patrol car and then heads towards the door of the shop.

In the donut shop, several customers are seated in booths or at tables drinking coffee and munching donuts. Carlyle is in a booth eating a cream filled donut. Cream squirts out as he bites it causing him to lean forward, but a gob of cream lands on his tie. With exaggerated movements, Carlyle places the donut on a plate and then picks up a napkin as he mutters to himself.

"God moves in mysterious ways," says Billings as he approaches the booth and Carlyle.

Carlyle looks up from his tie, "Screw you, Billings., If Millie finds out, I'll know who told her."

"Ah my friend, there's enough cream on that silk tie I won't have to tell her."

Billings takes a seat in the booth, on the opposite side. Carlyle dips his napkin in a glass of water and frantically scrubs at the spot on his tie; leaving pieces of wet napkin. Carlyle whines, "Ah crap. Millie bought me this; I can't just throw it away." Carlyle stops scrubbing; he speaks in a conspiratorial voice. "Why'd you drop that donut on me, Billings?"

"You buy the coffee, I'll take the blame."

Carlyle with a look of defeat takes another look at his stained tie. "I'll buy; but forget it, she'd never believe it." Carlyle waves a hand at the waitress for more coffee.

The waitress, a dyed blond of forty delivers an empty cup and a pot of coffee. She places the empty cup in front of Billings, fills it and then refills Carlyle's. In a smoker's voice she says, "Hey Billings, you come to save Carlyle? Millie finds out he's off his diet..."

"Ah come on, I'll leave you a nice tip," offers Carlyle.

"My lips are sealed, but that tie tells it all," laughs the waitress. She coyly winks at Billings.

Billings and Carlyle watch her rolling hips as she walks away.

Carlyle refocuses on his tie. Defeated, he shrugs his shoulders and picks up the donut.

Billings is once again focused on Carlyle, "Got a question for you."

Carlyle wipes his mouth with a napkin, "Yeah, what's that?" Carlyle licks cream from his fingers.

"Haven't you got an undercover used to be in the Marines?"

"Early, John Early; it was his wife got killed at the mall a while back."

"That was his wife, must have really messed him up."

"He adored her. Yeah, it tore him up; they were so excited about the baby." Carlyle wipes his fingers with a napkin, "Why, what's up?"

"Oh nothing, we were talking at the station, and it came up."

Carlyle's look of a kid sneaking a donut, quickly turns to a cop's look of suspicion, "Bullshit, what's up Billings, why do you want to know about Early?"

Billings lowers his voice, "You've heard about our crack pirates?"

"You mean the Vigilantes?"

Billings cringes and looks around to see if anyone has heard Carlyle. "Geeze, not so loud, but two guys, we believe are or were Marines, beat the crap out of three muggers today."

"I don't know if Early was involved, but he sure could have done it. He was Force Recon; he can be one bad dude."

"I was in the Corps; Force Recon is the cream of the tough guys."

"Yup, he and his brother-in-law were both in. It's how Early met his wife, she was Bear's sister."

"Who's this Bear? Nickname?"

You spell it B-e-h-r, which became The Bear; he's in town staying with Early."

Billings sits back and takes a sip of his coffee, thinking. He leans forward. "His brother-in-law came to Battle Creek because of his sister's death?"

That and help to Early; he's got Post Traumatic Stress Disorder; an ambush in Afghanistan killed everyone in his patrol but him. I understand he was listed as MIA."

"He was taken, prisoner?"

"No, he was wounded, and he'd tracked the ambushers to their camp and killed them. The rescue found him and fourteen dead Taliban; John had killed em all."

Billings, his hands wrapped around his coffee cup, sits without speaking for a few moments. In a sudden movement Billings pushes the cup away and gets out of the booth, "Gotta go."

Carlyle looks up at Billings. "I don't think Early is your guy. I don't know Bear, but John is one of the nicest people you'd ever want to meet."

Billings heads for the door, Carlyle calls out, "Hey, one more thing."

Billings stops and turns. "I'm telling Millie you dropped a donut on the tie."

"Yeah, yeah, your story's safe with me." Billings touches the brim of his hat with his forefinger.

Carlyle says seriously, "Keep safe my friend."

"Yeah, and you, see ya."

In the parking lot, Billings stands next to his patrol car absently patting his pockets. He thinks, 'Took out fourteen men because they killed his friends. I wonder what a man like that would do if someone killed his wife and child?' Billings finds his keys; and again, he stands looking over the top of the patrol car. Then he enters the car, starts it and rapidly exits the parking lot.

THE HOOD - EARLY'S SUV - NIGHT

The Bean and another man are walking up and down the sidewalk in front of a house. In the SUV, Bear and John listen on the scanners to Bean and the man talking.

"Remember, Smoke wants pickups each hour. You see anything, you call," says Bean.

The two Marines watch as Bean, and the man do a fist bump.

Bear starts the SUV, "Let's follow this guy. Maybe he'll lead us to Smoke."

They watch as Bean walks to his BMW and gets in. Bear waits till Bean pulls away and then follows the BMW down the street.

Bean's BMW makes a sudden right turn into a driveway and stops.

John says, "Break it off, break it off, he's checking for a tail. We'll figure something else out."

Bear flips on the turn signal, and then makes a turn at the corner.

Bean watches the SUV pass by, sees the blinker come on, and then make a right turn and out of sight. Bean backs out of the drive and heads in the opposite direction.

SMOKE'S HOUSE - LATER

Smoke sits in a recliner, Bean is standing. Smoke is all business, as he listens to Bean.

"We've shut down all but two houses. The duo is figuring out a place to wait for them Vigilantes."

"You make sure you do pickups every hour. I don't want any more money or product going out the door."

"Any luck at all, Smoke, the duo will take em out soon."

"To hell with luck; Detroit is pissed, and our asses are in a sling if we don't get these guys. Do you understand that? They will waste us if we don't straighten this shit out."

"The duo's got a plan, they'll get em."

* * *

Black-man and Rob-em, are dressed in SWAT type clothing, black ski masks are rolled up on top of their heads. They are in the prone position in a vacant lot, tall grass and junk surround them as they watch a house through night vision goggles. The house is located on the far side of the lot. People are coming and going from the house. Loud music can be heard.

In front of the house are two guards. In back is another guard, who is more interested in his cell phone, than guarding the back door. Black-man whispers to Rob-em, "Man this sucks. I ain't never see so many bugs, and they all seem to like dark meat, and that sweet smell... what the hell is that all about?"

"Cereal replies Rob-em, they're making cereal at one of the factories."

"If this doesn't work in a day or two, we'll try something else. Detroit says if we don't get these guys soon, we're to take out Smoke and his skinny partner."

"Rob-em goes on alert; "Left front, side of the house, see him?"

Black-man sees through the green light of his night vision, a man dressed in SWAT clothing, in a crouched position, moving toward the back of the crack house. "There's number two behind him. They're headed for the guard at the back door."

The two assassins watch as the two figures move towards the back door and the guard. The guard is texting on his cell phone, unaware of his surroundings. The men quickly take the guard down.

Black-man claps his hand on the shoulder of Rob-em, "Ok, let's go earn our money."

Black-man and Rob-em, stand, take off their goggles, and pull their ski masks down. They quickly put their night vision goggles back on and rapidly move towards the crack house.

At the back of the drug house, the backdoor guard squirms as plastic cuffs are placed around his wrists. Black-man and Rob-em attack the two men on top of the guard.

The guard is crazy with fear as two masked bodies fall next to him and don't move. The guard nearly losses his mind when multiple shots can be heard inside the house followed by screams.

* * *

Police cars, with lights flashing, are parked in front of the drug house. People in handcuffs are being led away by uniformed officers.

The SWAT Commander, a muscular man in a black jumpsuit, heavy body armor, helmet, and an MP-5 slung across his chest, watches as a vehicle arrives.

The CSI parks his car, exits, and heads toward the house.

The Commander's attention is drawn back to the street when another patrol car arrives. Galloway parks his patrol car; watches as the

CSI enter the crack house. Galloway spots the SWAT Commander. Getting out of his patrol car, Galloway starts speaking, as he strides towards the commander, "What the hell happened?"

"We've got two of our guys on their way to the hospital."

Galloway interrupts, "Shot?"

"No, their biggest injury is to their pride. They both have fat lips and a dollar's worth of nickel knots on their heads." Commander pulls a notebook from his vest pocket and begins to read. "Total, we shot one armed banger. Arrested ten, seven in the house and three in back, two of which, we thought were the Vigilantes."

Galloway becomes agitated by the comment, "You thought? You'd better talk me through from the beginning."

The commander takes a moment to gather his thoughts. "We had a warrant for the house. Surveillance told us that there were two guards in the front and one in back. The Commander points toward the back of the house. "We took down the two guards in front. When we got the"Go" signal from the backdoor-team, we hit the front door.

The Commander motions for Galloway to follow him to the back of the house. He continues talking as they walk. "When things calmed down we noticed that we were missing our two men from the back. Galloway and the Commander walk around the corner of the back of the house.

The Commander points at the ground with the light of his flashlight. "We found them cuffed there, along with the backdoor guard and two unidentified men in SWAT type uniforms."

Galloway is incredulous, as he listens to the report. "Your men were cuffed?"

"And three others; the Backdoor guys took down the guard and had just given the"Go," when they were jumped by two unidentified men."

Frustrated, Galloway blurts out, "Well what the hell happened..."

Billings comes out the back door of the crack house and interrupts Galloway, "Well L.T., looks like the Vigilantes have struck again, but this time we may owe em one."

Galloway fishes out his smokes. The SWAT Commander and Billings step back, as he lights up.

Galloway frowns at the two men. He takes a deep drag on his smoke, tilts his head back, and then blows the smoke into the night sky.

"The two in jail had murder on their minds. They were here to make a hit on the Vigilantes," said Billings.

"You think they mistook our men for…"

"The Vigilantes," interrupts Billings. "I think the Vigilantes jumped the bad guys and left them for us."

"How can you be sure it was them?"

"The guard, our guys, and the two in jail, all had smiley faces stuck to their foreheads."

Galloway throws down his smoke, grinds it into the ground. He pulls out a foil packet of antacids from his pocket. Popping two into his mouth, he chews while thinking.

"I'll meet you both at the office after I talk to CSI."

MOTEL ROOM - LATER

John and Bear are watching the news on TV, a newscaster says, "In the local news, the Police Department reported a police-involved shooting this evening while serving a warrant. The dead man has not yet been identified." Bear clicks the TV off, stands and stretches, "Nothing new on the news."

John stands, stretches, walks to a window, pulls back the drapes and looks out. He lets go of the drapes and turns to Bear. "The two we took out tonight... they were there to take us out."

"Good thing we had our listening devices out. I wonder if we would have spotted them."

"The police surveillance never spotted them, and the bad guys didn't recognize the PD, or they'd have known it wasn't us by the house."

"Well, we know who they work for and that's Smoke. We have to find out what Smoke looks like, and where he hangs out."

"The skinny banger they call Bean, if we continue watching him we'll find Smoke."

"I've got an idea. Remember Nowak, when he got out, he opened a store in New York, selling surveillance gear. He's got a website; we can get his number and call him. I bet he's got some goodies we can use to track these guys."

"Sounds good, in the morning we'll go back to the house and use the computer."

VA HOSPITAL - SECRETARY'S DESK

Sergeant Billings is sitting in the waiting area of Doctor Smith's office. Billings watches as the secretary answers her phone. She hangs up and addresses Billings. "Officer, Doctor Smith will see you now."

Billings stands. "Go in, he's waiting," the secretary says.

"Thank you." Billings knocks on the door and enters. Doctor Smith is sitting behind his desk. "Thank you for seeing me on short notice."

"Please, have a seat. The VA police said you're investigating Sergeant Early?"

Billings takes the seat in front of Smith's desk. He pulls out his notebook and flips through the pages. "Yes sir, Mr. Early has come to our attention. I'm trying to get some background on him, and any insight you can give me."

"Yes of course. Sergeant Early came under my care approximately two years ago..."

GALLOWAY'S OFFICE - LATER

Galloway is rocking in his swivel chair, gazing out the window. Behind him, seen through the door, plainclothes detectives and uniformed officers are busy with paperwork and phones.

Galloway turns his chair to the desk and picks up a thick file folder. He leafs through the pages without looking at them, his mind dulled.

Billings stands in the doorway and knocks. Galloway waves him into the office.

"I hope you've got more than I have," says Galloway.

Billings remains standing, while he pulls his notebook from his shirt pocket. He shuffles through the pages until he finds what he wants. "Okay, I went out to the VA and talked to a Doctor Smith. Turns out John Early is a former Marine with two hands full of medals." Billings continues to read, as he moves to the chair in front of the desk, he sits down. "Two of those medals cost him a trip to Great Lakes Naval Hospital. One for wounds received the other for valor."

Galloway asks, "Where'd this take place?"

"Afghanistan, he was leading a DRP when they were ambushed. Boss I gotta tell you the Recon guys were bad asses, tough as hell, very loyal to each other, trained in the extreme."

"DRP?"

It stands for Deep Recon Patrol. Everyone was killed in an ambush but Early. The doc says Early lost it when he saw all of his buddies dead."

As Billings speaks of the ambush, Galloway remembers himself as a young Army Lieutenant. Galloway is terrified and is curled up in the fetal position as green tracers fly overhead, and RPG's explode around them. Galloway has been wounded, and his men are being shot to hell all around him. Beside him, a man-child soldier fires an M-60 machine gun into the jungle. The machine gunner is shot and slumps onto Galloway. Panicked, Galloway rolls away and then looks into the dying eyes of the wounded gunner. Blood pours from the gaping mouth of the gunner as he tries to speak to Galloway.

Galloway cries out in anguish. With tears streaming down his face, he picks up the machine gun and stands. Then firing from the hip, he charges the enemy. His men seeing their Lieutenant, rally, stand and charge, following Galloway into the jungle.

Shaken, Galloway quickly turns in his chair and stares out the window. He has not had a flashback in many months. He thinks about himself, then wonders if Early suffers from them.

Billings is flipping the pages of his notebook; he finds what he's looking for, "After his release from the VA, Early went to work for Carlyle and Associates as an undercover." Billings stops reading, looks up at Galloway's back.

Galloway turns back to Billings, tilts back in his chair. He has a distant, melancholy look in his eyes. Billings studies Galloway's face, then he continues, "Early's wife was the pregnant girl who was killed at a few months ago.

Still shaken, Galloway looks down and casually opens a file on his desk.

"Carlyle told me Early used the VA for counseling. Doc says he hasn't seen Early since his release over a year ago." Billings puts away his notebook.

Galloway looks up, he's regained his composure. "What about the other man, where's he fit in?"

"He's Early's brother-in-law, A.K.A. the Bear. The last name spelled B - E -H - R, is also a former Marine. Both born and raised in Kentucky."

Galloway sits up in his chair, his mood changes. "Well trained, southern accents and motive. Do we know where these guys are?"

"Early has a condo out at St. Mary's Lake." Billings lays an I.D. photo of Early on the desk. "I got a photo of Early from the V.A. police. We don't have anything on Bear yet."

Galloway picks up the photo, looks at it, and then hands it back. "You get a surveillance team out to St. Mary's Lake. I'll work on a warrant."

A STREET IN THE HOOD

John and Bear are in the SUV, John is behind the wheel. On the seat between them, is a Tablet, a small metal box with a short antenna and a roll of duct tape. They are watching several men standing in front of a house, talking. At the curb in front of the house, is Bean's black BMW.

The door of the house opens, and Bean steps out. He stops and speaks with the group in front of the house. Bean then goes to the BMW, gets in and drives away. Early and Bear follow at a distance.

Bean pulls up in front of another house. The street area is dark except for a streetlight several houses up. Bean exits the BMW and enters the house. Early and Bear park on the dark side of the streetlight. John says to Bear, "It's now or never."

Bear grabs the metal box and the duct tape and gets out of the SUV.

John watches, as Bear moves quickly through the shadows, to the back of Bean's BMW. Bear drops to the ground then onto his back and slides under the car. His legs protrude from under the car.

Bear, under the car, is taping the box to the undercarriage of the BMW. He burns his knuckles on the hot muffler but continues to work.

Moments later, Bean comes out the front door of the house. Bear is still under the car.

John sees Bean and pulls his pistol; he lays it on the seat next to him but stays in the car.

As Bean approaches the BMW, John watches as Bear's legs slowly disappear under the car.

Bean stops, looks around. John picks up his pistol. Bean looks up the street at the SUV partially hidden in the dark. He watches a moment, and then gets into the BMW and drives away.

As the BMW pulls away, Bear, his body now fully exposed, rolls into the shadow of the curb.

Bean looks into the rear-view mirror. Only the dark street can be seen, and the SUV stays parked. The BMW turns at the corner and then disappears.

Bear stands, and staying in the shadows, he jogs back to the SUV and gets in. As soon as he enters, John drives away.

John begins sniffing the air.

Bear sniffs the air. Bear whines, "Ah, shit."

Grinning John replies, "Man, you got that right. What the hell did you roll in?"

Bear looks at a stain on the sleeve of his hoodie. He pulls his hoodie off, rolls down the window and throws it out the window. He rolls the window back up.

John is grinning ear to ear. Bear gives John the finger, but he's laughing.

Bear picks up the tablet. He turns it on and then taps an icon. On the screen, a map appears. On the map is a green dot. The green dot is moving across the screen. "Got him, we have a strong signal."

John, driving, sniffs the air again. He reaches over, and pats Bear on the shoulder. "You know, a sure cure for that would be toilet paper." Bear watching the tablet screen, silently flips John a second bird. The SUV disappears into the night.

MIDDLE-CLASS NEIGHBORHOOD - DAY

Parked at the curb in front of a ranch style house is a red, compact car, with dark tinted windows. A "FOR SALE" sign is in the window. Early and Bear are talking to a kid in his late teens, who is dressed and acting like a wannabe banger. Parked behind the red car is Early's SUV.

John is kicking tires as Bear sticks his head into the car through the open driver's side window. Behr pulls his head out, a frown on his face. "Smells like a French elevator in there. What is that crap?"

"You mean the air freshener?"

"If that's fresher than the air that was in there, what the hell were you doing?"

The kid cops an attitude, but before he can get into it with Bear, John butts in. "How much do you want for it?"

The kid tries to regain his loss of face. "Twenty-five hundred, it's a good car."

"I'll give you two, cash right now."

The kid drops the attitude, "Done," he says.

Bear shakes his head, as he watches John walk to the SUV, opens the door and retrieves money from an envelope. He returns to the kid and counts out the money. "You got the pink?"

The kid pulls a wallet out of his back pocket and retrieves the pink slip for the car. He moves to the car, takes a pen from his shirt pocket and fills out the paperwork on the top of the car. He hands the pink slip and the keys to John.

John looks at the pink slip handed to him by the kid and stuffs it into his shirt pocket. He turns to Bear. "You drive the SUV; I'll meet you at the house."

EARLY'S CONDO - LATER

John and Bear are in the living room. Two duffel bags are on the couch; both Bear and John are packing personal items into the bags.

"We leave the SUV?"

"Yeah, we'll head out when we're done. I booked our flight on the computer; we fly out of Grand Rapids. Bear smiles, as he continues to pack.

ST. MARY'S LAKE - EARLY'S CONDO SEVERAL HOURS LATER

In the driveway is the SUV. Down the street, parked in front of several parked cars is an unmarked police car. A two-man surveillance team listens to the radio traffic as they watch the condo. Over the police radio, the dispatcher is talking, "The SUV is registered to a J. K. Early."

The detective in the passenger seat picks up the mike and responds, "10-4 dispatch." He then picks up a cell phone and speed dials a number. "Yeah L.T., this is Barns...

GALLOWAY'S OFFICE

Galloway looks up as Billings enters the room and says, "Nothing so far at the condo; surveillance did see a ballistic vest in the back of the SUV with a bullet hole in it.

"I've got additional info back on Early, he owns two Par-Ordinance forty-fives."

"Make sure everyone has a photo of Early and a description of Bear. Did you tell Carlyle to contact you if he hears from Early?

"Yeah, I told him, but I've saved the best for last. Carlyle told me Early's Recon team? They pasted smiley faces on enemy soldiers they'd taken out."

Galloway stands and slaps his hands on the desk. "Got em, we've got em!"

THE HOOD

Bean is slouched in the driver's seat, driving his BMW. As he makes quick turns, he checks the side and rearview mirrors for a tail. Bean makes a tire-squealing U-turn and then a quick right onto a dark street. He turns into the driveway of an old two-story house with the paint chipping off. Bean parks in the drive. He retrieves a gym bag from the front seat and then gets out of the car. Closing the door, he stands listening. Off in the distance, a dog is barking. Bean, heads to the back door of the house. He opens the back door and enters.

Smoke is sitting on a couch playing a video game, on a huge flat screened TV. Bean holds up the gym bag for Smoke to see, "Got another ten K here." Bean places the bag on the floor.

Smoke talks, as he plays the game. On the screen, people are being shot and blown up. Bean stands and watches Smoke play. "Detroit's sending a crew to get the money tomorrow. You hear anything about our so-called Dynamic Duo?"

"Ain't heard shit man, but I do know the cops are looking for two white guys; been showing a picture around."

"Get me one of those pics; I want to see if I recognize this dude." Smoke continues to play as Bean leaves.

RED, COMPACT CAR

Bear is driving, because of his size he looks like he's been stuffed in behind the steering wheel.

John is in the passenger seat, he's holding the tablet on his lap.

"I feel like a pimp riding in this," says John.

"It was your idea, wouldn't be bad weren't for that damned air freshener; throw it out.

John reaches over and grabs the air freshener hanging from rear view mirror and gives it a jerk. The mirror comes off along with the air freshener. John, with a lopsided grin, holds it up by the unbroken string for Bear to see.

"Quit tearing up the car and check the tablet," growls Bear.

After tossing the mirror onto the floor, John turns on the tablet and then touches an icon. On the screen, a map of Battle Creek appears along with green dot on the map. "He's stopped, looks like the same place as last night."

John points as their car passes Smoke's house. "There, there behind the house. I can see the back of his Beamer."

Bear turns into a driveway; stops, backs out on to the street, and then heads back the way they came. "I saw a place we can park back a couple blocks. We'll walk back and have a look-see."

Several minutes later, Bear and John return, dressed in dark clothing, with black watch caps pulled down to their eyes. A house across the street from Smoke's has a driveway lined with tall flowering bushes. The windows and doors are boarded up with plywood. Bear and Early look around, and then quickly move up the driveway, disappearing into the shadows.

Bear and Early sit hidden in the bushes surrounded by flowers, listening to the night.

John and Bear each remove a night vision monocular from the cargo pockets of their trousers. Again, they listen and begin watching the house.

* * *

A patrol car passes by the parked, red car. Patrolman Carter, a cheerful young man, sees the red car. It draws his attention, and he stops. Carter exits his patrol car and begins to check the red car when the police dispatcher's voice comes over his portable radio. Dispatcher, "All units, district three, eleven ninety-nine, officer needs help, Pat and Charlie's Bar."

Carter hurriedly writes the red car's plate number on the palm of his hand, and then gets into his patrol car and speeds away with red lights flashing.

MOTEL ROOM - DAY

John has a large duffel bag open on the suitcase stand. He removes two pistols, body armor, and places them on the floor and the bed next to black clothing. Bear is taking off his shirt, "I'm going to take a shower."

"Roger that, I'll get our stuff together for tonight, and then I'll take one." Bear leaves the room.

John pulls out one of the pistols and sits in a chair. He strips down the pistol and begins to wipe it down. John stops cleaning the pistol and picks up the TV clicker and turns on the TV. An infomercial is on. The woman speaking resembles Kay, triggering a memory. The sun is beginning to set. It's an idyllic evening. John sits in a deck chair. Next to him is a wooden table. There is a bird book on the table. Looking out at the lake, his face has a look of melancholy, he appears lost in thought.

Kay stands at the sliding glass door watching her husband. She opens the sliding glass door and steps out onto the deck. John looks up into her face, she smiles, "Hi sweetheart, are you OK?

"I'm fine, waiting for the geese to fly in."

Kay sits on his lap, her arms around his neck. She kisses him on the forehead, her soft lips lingering, and says "I love you." John hugs her.

Out on the lake, geese begin calling, Kay and John look towards the lake. A noisy flock of geese circles the lake, and as a group they land on the lake.

Kay says, "Several of them came up into the yard this morning. They reminded me of farm women wearing their babushkas and black rubber boots."

"I was reading about them. During the hunting season, if one gets shot, the mate will return, sacrificing its life for its fallen mate."

"Well, no one is going to hunt here. Our geese are safe. Besides," Kay pats her swollen stomach, "we have you to protect us."

Early, is stressed by the flashback, and grabs the TV clicker and turns off the TV. The bathroom door opens, and Bear enters drying his head with a towel. He doesn't notice the state his friend is in. "You gonna take a shower?"

John stands and moves towards the bathroom. "Yeah, I got to watching TV, didn't get much done."

"I'll get it. Tonight's the night bro. We take Smoke down and then head for Columbia."

John stops, turns to Bear, "Yeah, tonight's the night." He steps into the bathroom and closes the door.

Bear goes to the bags. He picks one up then notices the phone. Next to the phone is his wallet. He stops, hesitates, and then he sets the bag down and sits on the bed. Bear picks up his wallet. He looks at the photograph of him and Carlotta. He pulls a slip of folded paper from behind the photograph and unfolds it. Picking up the phone; he stops, looks at the time, smiles and starts dialing.

Carlotta has just taken a bath and is drying her hair with a towel. The phone rings. She drapes the towel around her neck and answers the phone, "Hello?"

"Hello, beautiful."

Carlotta is excited about hearing Bear's voice, almost beside herself with happiness, "You are coming home?"

"Yes, two days and I'll be home."

"Oh, my Big Bear, I miss you so."

"Just a couple of things to take care of and we'll be on the plane." Your friend, he comes too?

"Yes, he is coming too. Then no more will we be apart, you and me."

Happy, Carlotta sits on the side of the bed, and then lays back, the phone to her ear. "I love you, you come home; I will be waiting."

"I love you too. See you soon."

PATROL CAR - EVENING

Billings is parked so he can watch traffic as he writes in his patrol log. Finished, he pushes a button to close his door window; he picks up the radio mike.

"Dispatch contact the watch commander and have him meet Unit S-34 on the tactical channel scrambled."

Dispatch, "Ten-four, stand by one."

Billings pulls out his notebook leafing through the pages while he waits.

Dispatcher, "Unit S-34, W C will meet you on TAC three."

"Ten-four," Billings flips a switch on the radio. "Unit 34 is TAC three."

Billings, "TAC three."

GALLOWAY answers, "What have you got?"

"Suspects bought a car a couple of days ago, paid cash. The kid they bought it from had a picture of it. I'll get copies out ASAP."

"Copy that, I also heard from surveillance the perps have not returned to the condo."

"I doubt they'll go back, but you never know. I'm 10-19 to the office to copy the picture of the car."

"Roger that. I've got a couple of stops to make, and then I'll be back in the office."

Billings hangs up his mike, pulls out his cell phone and hits speed dial.

At Carlyle's office, the phone rings, Millie answers it, "Carlyle and Associates, how may I help you?"

"You can leave that husband of yours and run off to the Caribbean with me."

Millie's voice takes on an exaggerated southern-bell accent, "Why Sergeant Billings, I do declare, you're too forward! What would your lovely wife say if she knew how you talk?"

"Not a thing, she'd pull the trigger and walk away. Is your husband in?"

"No, but if you're calling about Early, he hasn't heard anything. Do you want him to call you?"

"No, only if he hears something. Thanks, Millie."

A half an hour later, Billings is making copies on a copy machine at the police station. Patrolman Carter walks by the door; he sees Billings. "Hey Sarge, whuzz up?"

Making copies for the patrols; "Before you go back out, stop and see me. I want you to get these out to the units."

"Roger that."

Fifteen minutes later, Carter finds Billings sitting at a desk. "I'm headed out, you got the copies?"

Billings picks up a stack of colored copies and hands them to Carter. "Make sure everyone gets one these. We think the Vigilantes are using this vehicle."

Carter takes the stack of copies; he looks at the top one. Surprise and excitement show on his face. "I saw this car last night."

Billings is also excited. "Did you get a plate number?"

Carter fishes in his shirt pocket and pulls out a notebook. "Michigan, B - B - Y - 443. I got called out on an 11-99 and didn't run the plate till later, it's stolen."

Billings copies the number into his notebook. "Carter, you get those out to the units ASAP."

DISPATCH OFFICE - MOMENTS LATER

Billings picks up a message pad from the dispatcher's desk. He copies information from his notebook to the pad. Billings pushes the pad to the dispatcher. "Broadcast this plate and vehicle description citywide, scrambled. Suspects are armed and dangerous." Billings starts to leave, stops and returns to the dispatcher. "No one stops the suspects without a backup on the scene. Emphasize that, backup is to be on the scene, not rolling before a stop is attempted."

The dispatcher writes down the additional information on the pad and then keys her mike. "All units switch to TAC two scrambled..."

Billings pulls out his cell phone and hits speed dial.

"Carter, I'll meet you where you last saw the suspects' vehicle, in about ten."

TWO PATROL CARS

Billings and Carter are parked driver's door to driver's door, windows down, "Hey Sarge, kinda slow tonight."

"Don't jinx it, Carter, by talking about it."

"You know Sarge, I've been thinking; Smoke lives a couple of blocks over."

Billings shouts, "Gotta go!" As he puts his vehicle into gear Billings leans out the window, "Good work Carter, damn good work."

Carter, a questioning expression on his face, watches as Billings speeds off. Billings pulls his cell phone and speed dials. "Dispatch, contact Galloway, and the SWAT commander. Tell them we'll need SWAT, ASAP. Advise them I'll meet them in the Watch Commander's office."

POLICE STATION - MEETING ROOM

Galloway, Billings, SWAT Commander, and the Chief of Police, are all in the room. On the wall is a large satellite map of the city. Galloway, addressing the SWAT commander, points to the map and a block of houses. "This is Smoke's house. From past surveillance, we can give you the layout for your SWAT team."

The SWAT Commander moves closer and points to the map. "I'll station our wagon here. We'll be out of sight of the house."

"The surveillance team will be in this empty house across the street," Galloway tells the Commander.

With a frown, the Commander says, "I wish we had more time on this."

Galloway, Yeah, me too, but if these guys come calling tonight, it could become a battle royal. Chief, you got anything?"

"Commander, you have the green light to do what's necessary. These are highly trained men who will kill without hesitation."

"Yes sir, I understand."

"Okay," says the Chief, "let's get it moving."

VACANT TWO-STORY HOUSE - LATER

A two-man surveillance team in plain clothes is stationed at the upstairs' front windows. The room is lighted by ambient light from streetlights outside. Both men have night vision, binoculars, and walkie-talkies.

Team Member #1 speaks into a handheld radio, "I have two male subjects approaching from the West; North side of the street."

On the sidewalk, John and Bear, their hoodies hiding their faces, unaware they are being watched, pass in front of the surveillance house.

SWAT VAN

The SWAT Commander listens to the radio chatter about the two bangers. In the back of the van the SWAT Team is displaying nervous anticipation as they listen to the radio.

VACANT HOUSE - SURVEILLANCE TEAM

TEAM MEMBER #1 on the radio, "The two subjects have passed the target and are continuing down the street."

John and Bear continue up the street past the surveillance house. In a dark spot they duck into the shadows of the trees that line the street. They stand together listening for any unusual night sounds. John signals for Bear to go, and in turn they sprint across the street staying in the shadow of a light pole. The two men stop in the shadows of a house and again listen. They move up into a driveway between two houses.

Early and Bear begin scaling fences and running through backyards, back towards Smoke's house. They are lucky and no dogs bark at them.

MOMENTS LATER

Bear and John crouch in the shadows listening, hearing no abnormalities, no conversations between hidden guards, nothing. On the move again, they head toward the back door of Smoke's house. They are nearly caught in the headlights of a car entering the driveway. Early and Bear just make it into the shadows as Bean drives up the driveway and parks his Beamer. Bean gets out of the car, in his hand is a picture of John Early. Bean enters the house.

Inside, Smoke is watching two men as they finish running bills through an electronic counter. They take the stacks of money, wrap rubber bands around them and place the stacks into a large duffel bag. Bean enters the room from the back door.

"It cost me a couple of rocks, but I got one of the crack heads to take it out of a cop car." Bean hands the picture to Smoke.

"Good Bean, you did good." As Smoke takes the photo, the back door is kicked open. John and Bear, guns in hand rush through the door. The money counters jump up from the table, drawing their guns. Bean and Smoke also pull their guns. Everyone begins shooting.

SWAT VAN

TEAM MEMBER #1, "Shots fired! Shots fired!"

The Commander slaps his palm on the dash. He shouts, "Go, go, go!"

The van speeds up the street. Inside the van, the SWAT team braces, as the van accelerates and turns corners. The commander begins the countdown. "Stand-by... Two hundred yards... Seventy... Ready!" The Van comes to a halt in front of Smoke's house.

The Commander gives the order, "Go, go, go!"

The back doors of the van burst open, and the two SWAT teams hit the street running. The teams split, one going to the front door of Smoke's house. The second team moves rapidly up the drive to the back door of the house. Multiple shots can be heard coming from the house.

SMOKE'S HOUSE

Smoke dives to the floor, rolls and comes up shooting. Bean shoots at Bear and drops to the floor. John shoots and kills Bean. The two Detroit men drop behind the table and begin firing at Bear and John. Bear is hit in the chest, and staggers back but still fires his weapon. He extends his forefinger out straight and against the trigger while locking his arm steady against his body. He rapidly moves his finger back and forth firing his pistol like a machine gun.

Bullets tear up the table and floor, the Detroit men die in the hail of bullets. Bear ejects the empty magazine and reloads.

Bear is shot in the legs by Smoke. Bear drops to the floor, an artery has been cut in his leg, and he begins to bleed out. Frantically, he tries to stop the bleeding. Early changes magazines as he steps over Bear and takes up a protective position over him, continuing his firing.

Smoke rolls across the floor and raises his pistol with a bloody hand to shoot John, but he freezes, a look of surprise on his face. "You," shouts Smoke, It's you."

Time stops as the two men stare at each other. Recognition floods John's face.

PARKING LOT – MONTHS AGO

John is getting out of his SUV. Parked next to him is Smoke's car. On the far side of the car, Smoke is bent over looking at a scratch in the paint of his car. As Smoke stands, his head becomes visible. John comes around his car just as Smoke's head pops up from behind his car. Smoke, angry about the scratch, swears. John is startled as he sees Smoke's head come up from behind the car. John imagines Smoke as an Arab. Drawing his pistol, John begins firing at an Arab combatant.

The Arab draws his pistol and begins shooting but is overwhelmed by Early's shooting. The Arab takes cover behind a rock.

Smoke is in his car speeding out of the parking lot. A bewildered John Early looks around. Police sirens bring him back to reality, he gets into his car and speeds away.

In the house, Smoke points his pistol at the stunned John Early. John, his pistol pointed at Smoke, is unable to pull the trigger, he's frozen in place. Tears begin rolling down his cheeks, his hands shake, and then his body.

From the floor, between Early's legs, Bear raises his pistol and fires round after round into Smoke. Smoke's body jerks from Bear's shots, Smoke fires one last shot that strikes Bear in the head, killing him. Smoke dies simultaneously with Bear.

An explosion at the front door blows it off its hinges, the SWAT team enters the room.

At the back door, the second SWAT team enters; the commander points his MP-5 at Early. "Down, down, drop the gun, drop the gun!"

Early, his pistol still pointed at the dead Smoke, is frozen in place, he's looking at the carnage in the room. Red dots from laser sights cover his body. John looks down at Bear, dead at his feet.

"Put the gun down, put down the gun!"

In one swift motion, John turns the pistol and points it under his chin. In disbelief, the Commander and the SWAT team watch as Early commits suicide. John Early collapses to the floor next to Bear.

EARLY'S CONDO - EVENING

Galloway and Billings are standing on the deck. The sun is setting. Behind them, uniformed police can be seen through the sliding glass doors searching the house. Inside the house the phone rings, the officers look at each other. One of the officers picks up the phone.

"Hello?" He cups his hand over the mouthpiece. "Anyone speak Spanish?"

An officer steps up to the phone and takes it. He listens a moment and the hands it back. "Whoever it was, they hung up."

On the deck, Billings and Galloway watch a flock of geese circle the lake calling and then gliding in and landing on the water. One goose stays in the air, circling and calling.

Galloway reaches into his shirt pocket and takes out his smokes. The package is empty.

Billings says, "Good time to quit."

Galloway crumples the empty pack and starts to throw it on the deck, thinks better of it, and puts it in his pocket. He looks out over the lake. The lone goose still circles, it's plaintive call echoing across the lake.

"Did you get the ballistics back on the guns?"

"Yeah, it was Early's, it was his gun that killed his wife."

"How do you figure it?"

Billings leans on the railing of the deck, "I think Early was in the parking lot. Smoke just happened to be there. We'll never know for sure what really happened."

Billings moves to the railing of the deck next to Galloway. They watch the lone goose circling, calling. Billings continues, "Early may have stopped taking his meds, which can cause flashbacks. His mind couldn't accept the realization that he'd killed his wife."

Galloway replies, "When he saw Smoke it must have all come back." He wonders what John Early saw in his head in those last few seconds. He wonders if the vision he had in the office will return.

Galloway again watches the solitary goose flying over the lake, calling. "My dad used to hunt. One day a short time after he returned from WWII, he shot a goose on our farm. For days its mate returned, calling, looking for its mate. A few days later, Dad found it dead by the pond. He never hunted again.

THE END

About the Author

John was born in February of 1941 and raised in Flint, Michigan. His was a middle-class family. His father was a musician and a radio disk jockey. His mother wrote short stories and radio scripts. His mother and father had a Sunday afternoon radio program. His mother wrote the scripts, and both parents played the different characters.

As a teen, John worked at a gun shop and learned a great deal about weapons, hunting, and shooting. He became an instructor for shooting skeet and trap. John came in second as junior state champion. This training came in handy when he joined the Marines in 1959 after high school.

In the Marines, John graduated boot camp with promotion and sent to Camp Pendleton to work as a small arms repairman. He attended several weapons classes, always finishing in the top ten in his class.

John later was assigned to a guard company in Guam. During this tour, John and another marine were involved in a prolonged gunfight with six intruders in a highly restricted area. They captured five of the intruders and the sixth was arrested the next day. They were given letters of accommodation for "Prompt and heroic action while in a restricted area." John returned to the states just in time to be deployed to Cuba during the Cuban Missile Crisis. Upon his return from Cuba, John was honorably discharged.

John spent the next several years working in law enforcement in California. He was a city officer, federal officer, and a deputy. Police officers did not make a great deal of money back then. By now John was married with two children. He began working in heavy construction as a teamster driving the big heavy trucks you often see in mining. During this time the family decided to move back to Michigan. Unlike California, construction work in Michigan was seasonal, so he sought a more stable job.

John found it in foundry work. He began work as a mold maker and eventually worked his way up to superintendent of a three shift 210 man shop. It was during this time that he saw a business opportunity.

John wrote a business plan for a security patrol. The business started out with three employees and two patrol vehicles. In a short period, it grew to 110 employees, with a superbly trained team of bodyguards. The business expanded into international sales of equipment. During this time John attended schools and became certified as a bodyguard and a security driver. His company protected high profile people from executives to visiting royalty. They also contracted to investigate drugs in the workplace and internal theft, working closely with local and state agencies.

The security business required John to travel across the United States, Europe, Japan, Korea, and the Middle East. He met and worked with men and women of different Special Forces from around the world, and law enforcement. John met and befriended high officials in Eastern Europe many of whom he still communicates.

John sold the business several years ago and retired to Las Vegas, Nevada. He began writing using his experiences and knowledge of the military and police. John has written two novels, "The House of Crow" and "White Crow." John is finishing the third book of The House of Crow trilogy, "The Crow Legacy." A third published book, a novella, "With Deadly Purpose," is published and is also in audio.

* * *

To learn more about John W. Wood and discover more Next Chapter authors, visit our website at www.nextchapter.pub.

With Deadly Purpose
ISBN: 978-4-82412-633-7

Published by
Next Chapter
1-60-20 Minami-Otsuka
170-0005 Toshima-Ku, Tokyo
+818035793528
8th March 2022